Meet the Pups

Written by **Sheila Sweeny Higginson**

Based on the series created by **Travis Braun**

Designed by **David Roe**

DISNEP PRESS

Los Angeles • New York

Here are the pups.

They are a crew.

They like to build.

They have a job to do!

This is Phinny.

He is small.
He thinks big.

This is Luna.

She likes to dig.

This is Tank.

He is strong.

This is Roxy.

She bangs!
She crushes!

The crew gets a call.

They have a job to do.

The pups are ready!

They go to work!

Oh no!

A rock is in the way.

Roxy helps.

She bangs.

She crushes.

No luck.

Phinny has an idea.

Phinny thinks.

He draws.

He plans.

Luna digs.

Tank pours.

Roxy helps.

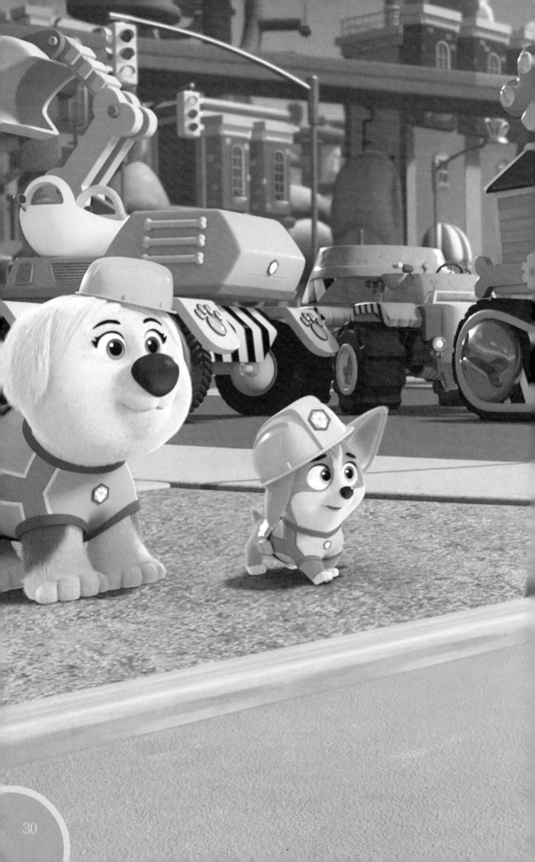

They have a job to do.

Good job!